To my mother, Ruth, who taught me how to wash clothes —M. S.

For the Richins family —T. B.

Text copyright © 2016 by MaryAnn Sundby
Illustrations copyright © 2016 by Tessa Blackham

First Edition 2016

Library of Congress Control Number 2016932258
ISBN 978-0-9913866-6-6

10 9 8 7 6 5 4 3 2 1
Printed in South Korea

This book was typeset in Didot.
The illustrations were rendered in hand-painted cut-paper collage.

Ripple Grove Press

Portland, OR
www.RippleGrovePress.com

Monday Is Wash Day

written by MaryAnn Sundby

illustrated by Tessa Blackham

Ripple Grove Press

Rain or shine, Monday is wash day.

Mama brags that Annie and I help do the wash.
"Can't I just go out and play?" I ask in my kindest voice.

"First we work and then we play." Mama smiles but
walks with purpose to the porch.

Annie and I gather shirts and pants
from the hampers and the closets.
We hunt for stray socks
under beds and behind doors.

That's how we help Mama make the laundry go away.

"I can lift more than you!" I tease Annie
as I carry clothes to the back porch.
We run back to the bedrooms
and gather more shirts and socks.

Our baby brother climbs onto the mountain of clothes.
From the top, he claps and cheers.

Next we sort the clothes just the way Mama thinks best.
"Whites go in a pile, lights in a pile, darks in a pile too.
First load is the whites, light clothes are next, and the darks are last."

How did we get so much so dirty?

We carry buckets of water to the back porch.
We pour hot water into the washer.
We pour cold water into the rinse tubs.

"I can lift more than you!" Annie teases me.

Mama measures the soap, and I toss it in. I look at Mama, and she smiles at me.
We switch on the old machine, and it squeaks and squawks while soap bubbles grow.

It sings, *round and back, round and back, I pound the dirt away.*

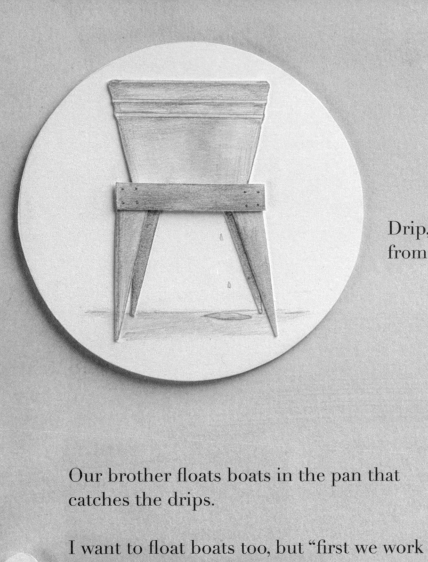

Drip, drip, drip splashes water to the floor
from a tiny leak at the bottom of a rinse tub.

Our brother floats boats in the pan that
catches the drips.

I want to float boats too, but "first we work
and then we play."

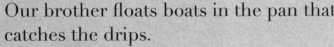

We lift heavy shirts and pants out of the soapy water.
We feed the shirts and pants through the wringer
to the first rinse tub.
The wringer squeezes the water out of the clothes.

Puddles grow. It's a mess.

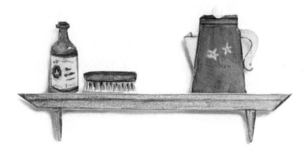

Mama pulls a bottle of bluing from a shelf.
"Our shirts might be thin, but they won't be dull and gray."

She untwists the cap of the stuff that makes white clothes look bright.
"Is it my turn to sprinkle in the bluing?" Annie asks.

She shakes a few drops into the water, and it becomes light blue.
A very pretty blue.

The clothes fall from the wringer into a tub of cold water.
We lift them up and down to get the soap out.
We put them into another rinse tub as cold water splashes out.
Again we lift the clothes up and down.

Mama claims that sand could still be hiding in our socks.
So we put our hands in the cold water and turn our socks inside out.

"You go first," I nudge Annie. Our hands ache from the cold water.
Our brother splashes his hands in the cold water and giggles with glee.

When Mama finally puts Daddy's work pants into the washer, Monday's wash is almost gone!
We carry the wet clothes to the clotheslines for the sun and wind to dry.

Soon Annie and I will go and play.

Our brother crawls in the grass around the clotheslines.
We hand clothespins to Mama as she shakes out the clothes and pins them to the line.

"Our neighbors won't see our socks and slips!" Annie and I giggle as Mama puts everything in a special order.

Sheets and towels on the outside line. Shirts and blouses on the middle line. Socks are to be placed close to the house. Our blouses pop like flags in the wind.

I pin my doll dresses on the line just like Mama pins up my dresses.
Mama beams with pride when our wash is hanging outside early on Monday morning.

When everything is hanging outside to dry, we clean up.
We help Mama drain water out of the tubs into our buckets.
We carry the buckets outside, but water splashes everywhere.
We water the thirsty flowers near the back door.

As the sun rises higher we run to Mama and say,
"It's time to gather in the clothes."

Annie and I wrap ourselves in the sheets and
smell their sweet scent. We fold our dresses and
the doll dresses on the kitchen table.

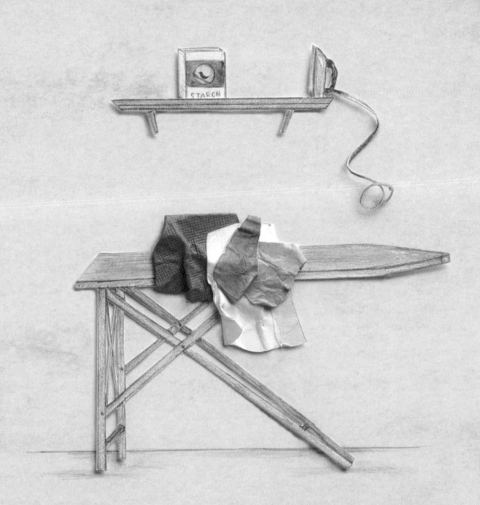

We carry the socks and shirts upstairs to drawers and closets.
We set aside the wrinkly shirts and pants for ironing day.

Mama smiles at Annie and me.
"Thanks to my helpers, our wash is done."

We waste no time. . . .

We go outside and play.

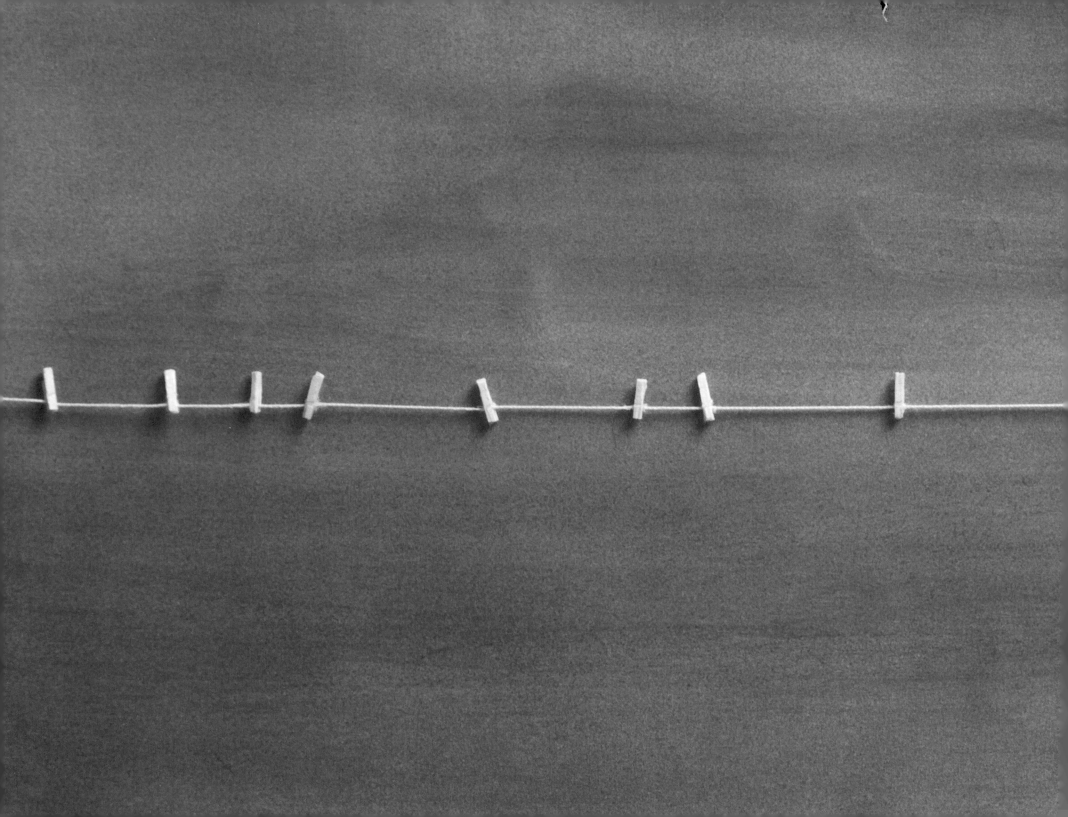